TEENY
LITTLE
GRIEF MACHINES

LINDA OATMAN HIGH

SADDLEBACK
EDUCATIONAL PUBLISHING

GRAVEL ROAD

SADDLEBACK
EDUCATIONAL PUBLISHING
www.sdlback.com

ISBN-13: 978-1-62250-883-9
ISBN-10: 1-62250-883-1
eBook: 978-1-61247-998-9

Printed in Guangzhou, China
NOR/0514/CA21400852

18 17 16 15 14   1 2 3 4 5

VERSE

DEDICATION

For the Highlights Foundation and my fellow poets
at the magical Novel in Verse workshop, where
ninety-five percent of this book was written.

PART ONE:

THE FALL

TICKING ... TOCKING

My name is Lexi
          (rhymes with sexy)
McLeen, sixteen,
          and this is what I

believe:

          we are each

Teeny Little
          Grief Machines ...

ticking ...
tocking ...

bombs
programmed to explode ...

if we have not

already

detonated.

My Entire Family Is a Disease

Dad: Alcoholic. Depressive.
Borderline Personality Disorder.

Stepmom: Anorexic. Anger Issues. Bipolar.

The two of them together:
hoarders of cigarettes
and lottery tickets
that never win.

Blaine: Autistic. ADHD.

And me:
artistic.

That's what *they* say
anyway.

I paint
in shades
of blue.

The poetry
is just so

        I

               don't

                        explode.

ONCE I CARVED H-A-T-E
ON MY ARM

With scissors.

Just the tip.

Skimming.

Slicing lightly.

A tiny silver nip
of skin.

They thought

I must be a

cutter,

but I wasn't.

There was no knife.

I just
hated
my
life.

IT ALL STARTED

After we lost
the Baby.

It wasn't our fault.
Carissa,
my little sister,

just died in her white crib
in my bedroom
one night.

Peacefully, in her sleep, all tucked in,
bundled, swaddled, surrounded by pink
princess bumper pads and soft fuzzy blankets.
She wasn't on her stomach.

I can still see her face, sweet,
pink-cheeked,
eyes closed, baby butterflied eyelashes like
tiny splayed paintbrushes wisping her face.
She wasn't breathing. I checked for breath.

Crib Death.

And I think she would have been
Normal
otherwise.

BED DEATH

She was so pretty,
that bitty little sister of mine.

Just three weeks lived;
now one year dead.

I can't get her no-breath
face out of my head.

Sometimes I wish
we'd all just

get

Bed Death.

Now I Lay Me Down to Sleep

In one big lump of sob and weep.

Why was she taken in the night?
And when do *I* get some morning light?

Mourning …
Light?

I know, right?

Sometimes …

Life …

Bites.

THE SENSORY DETAILS OF CARISSA GRACE

Carissa Grace
was her name.

Carissa Grace McLeen:
three weeks
newly seen
in this obscene
old world.

Sometimes at night,
before I get a chance

to fight
the intense
memories,

I get swept
into the sensory
details
of Carissa Grace.

(Sensory details
are cool tools
for poets
to use,

but I mostly choose
to try to forget
the sensory

when it comes to
my little sister.)

When I'm swept
into Memory Land,
though, like crumb specks
into the dustpan of nighttime sky,
I'm mostly flooded with
the love,
cuddling
warm and soft,
to nuzzle the Baby

next to my chest.

We slept together
on my bed once,
her small body pressed
against mine.

Me flat on my back,
Carissa snuggly belly,
two heartbeats,
baby head,

soft breath
against
my neck.

Wisps of duck-fuzz hair,
whispery lips, chubby,
nubby-footed pajamas.

Baby Magic
soap smell,
powdery, clean,
sweet.

That was Carissa Grace.

She smelled like angels,

as if she came straight
from another place.

I wish she'd stayed.

THE STEPMOM TANYA

The stepmom—Tanya—eventually
became even
more evilish
after Carissa
died.

Anorexia ate her
alive.

Her bipolar disorder
became even more
disorganized.

Plus she just
generally
sucks.

She's dumb,
and how can I trust

somebody

who can't even spell

anything

right?

TANYA'S LIST OF CHORES FOR LEXI

Sweep kichen floor.
Toylet needs cleaned more.
Wipe bathroom dore.

I wonder if Tanya
can spell the word
"whore."

i
really
don't
care

… anymore.

The Dad

Why would any grown man
get a tattoo of his baby's name
needle-inked into
his skin,

if he's never planning to pay
Attention

to that baby
anyway?

I have no clue.

Why would any grown man
drive a pickup truck drunk one day

if he doesn't want to pay
the price

of his immature mistake?

I have no clue.

I don't know what to do,
so I just paint his face …
dark blue.

The cell bars are dark
blue too.

Daughter of an Incarcerated Father

Jail	jail
no bail	no fail
no mail	no hope
from me	for me

I am now the daughter
of an incarcerated father.
They write advice
for people like me.

THE BROTHER

Blaine,
he's eight but delayed.
Way delayed.
Like majorly autistic-ADHD Delayed
with a capital *D*.

Blaine,
he's eight but wears disposable diapers to pee.

Blaine,
he doesn't know how to behave,
but it's not his fault.
He was made that way.

Blaine.
Sometimes I think he's just plain

insane.

Once he chased me with a knife.
Said he was going to chop me up,
so the doctor switched his medicine
again and put him on clozapine.
That's for schizophrenics with violent
tendencies, my semi-friend Zelda said.

Zelda's a walking, talking Google search. Yahoo!

I wish she could find the answers
for Blaine.

OPEN CLOSE

Open
Close
Open
Close

That's the refrigerator door
when Blaine's around.

Miss Bess the TSS says
that we need to just lock the

refrigerator to avoid the mess.

Once, Blaine cracked a dozen eggs
over his own head.

Open
Close
Open
Close

Blaine picks his toes.
He picks his nose.
We pick our battles.
Blaine also tattles.

WHAT BLAINE SAID

Is not exactly what happened.
You can't just trust
what Blaine says.

He ratted me out
last week.
Completely
narked on me.

"I see
Lexi
smoking a
cigarette," Blaine said
to his mama,
who is Tanya.

(*My* real mom is in Alabama.)

Blaine lies.
(Big surprise.)

A cigarette it was not.

I was smoking

Pot.

Real Life, Good-bye

I got
the weed
from Morgan Reed,
the number one
marijuana wheeler-dealer
in school.

I'm no fool.
I didn't buy it.

I traded a custom love
poem and a painting,
"from Morgan" (but *really* from me)
to this guy Josiah
she's crushing on,
and she gave me
weed in trade.

Morgan has it made.

Her brother Seth
(I've heard he's tough)
grows the stuff
in a cornfield behind their house,
and he makes some nice profits.

Morgan is now the Queen of Weed,
hotshot pot mafia chick.

Sick.

Only problem:

Weed = Illegal.
Me + Poetry + Painting for Morgan = "High"

School.

Real life,
good-bye.

Tattoo Haiku

I want a tattoo.
I don't know what I want yet.
It will hurt so good.

WHAT CHLOE KING SAID

The whole
Lexi-rhymes-with-sexy thing
started with Chloe King.

Chloe King is the Queen of Every
Thing. (Except for weed.)

That's what she believes.

Chloe King asked me one day
if Lexi is my real name.
I told her yes, because why

would anybody have Lexi
for a fake name anyway?

What Chloe King said next
was that Lexi
is a stripper name.

She said
that she bets
I dance around a pole
for money.

That is so
not funny.

THE MOM

My
real
mom
was
once
a
stripper,
I
hear.

I
heard
that
from
Dad
when
he
had
too
much
beer.

Carissa Was There

With a
whole head of hair.

She was in my dream,
breathing, never leaving

until I woke up.
Waking up sucks.

It felt like a visit
from Carissa.

Just my luck
that eventually
I'd wake up.

You know how at the end of
The Wizard of Oz

Dorothy says to all the farm dudes:
You were there! And you were there!

And you were there!

So was Oz a dream
or was it real? What's the deal?

Nobody knows. It totally blows.

All I know for sure
is that Carissa *was there*.

But now she is

Not.

END OF THE WORLD GIRL

There's this girl
in school
named Valerie Jewel.
I call her End of the World
Girl.

Valerie's dad is in the Army
far away, and she only sees
him on Skype every now

and then. She says he's always
dressed in camouflage,
and he looks
like a mirage
in the desert
on the screen.

Valerie says that her dad
told them a military secret,
which I really don't believe.

But anyway, Valerie's family
stocked up on 800 pounds of wheat,
600 cans of food, and hundreds of jugs
of water.

They also bought a shotgun
with a thousand rounds of ammunition.

End of the World Girl freaks people
out. But not me, not really,
because I sort of wish
the Apocalypse
would hit us.

And then it would
just be finished.

The Guidance Counselor Is My Friend

My best friend, not a semi.

Ms. Rose looks like her name:
dew-perked, misted,
shiny curtain of slick black hair

streaked this week with magenta.

Maybe I'd paint *her* pink
instead of blue,

because she's definitely the best color
in my whacked-out life.

I'm here again today
in her office that feels

like home is supposed
to feel.

Safe, a quiet place. Nobody
yelling. Nobody cursing. Nobody
rehearsing
for hell.

I tell
her about my dream.
How Carissa was there,
with a full head of hair,

and how really it's just
Insane Blaine in
my Alive Sibling Count.
Half-brother

from a different mother,
but then again,
Carissa was just a half too.

And I tell her about Tanya,
who just sucks,
And I tell her about how
my mom

was a teenager (freakin' sixteen!)
when she had me,

and now
I don't see her a lot,
but that doesn't actually suck,
not too much.

Because Alabama is so far
from Pennsylvania
anyway.

And then,
at
the end,

I tell her about Dad,

and where
he is

now.

AT LEAST

He's not in the Army
and serving now in war.

At least
he's not in the Air Force
and leaving us here to soar.

At least
he's not in the Marines
and heading off to fight.

At least
he's only in the county jail,

and I can forget at night.

Now and Then

Every now and then,
I wish I could just begin again.

Every now and then,
I wish they'd put me up
for adoption,
and I'd be given a
Perfect family.

Every now and then,
I wish they'd decided
to just end it—
before I was even born,
before life began to suck.

Every now and then,
I wish it would all
just
end.

THE TIME I TOOK TYLENOL

It wasn't about suicide.
Yikes!

I only took twenty-five.

I'm still alive.

I
    Was
        Just
            Trying
                To
                    Make
                        The
                            Pain
                                Stop.

Tanya called the cops.

Not the ambulance.

That tells you a lot

about

Tanya.

September Again

End of summer.

Bummer.

The fall was when
Carissa died.

I don't need to
be reminded,
but I am.

I *so* am.

It's fall

again.

TANYA GOES OUTSIDE TO SMOKE

And I'm supposed to
keep an eye
on Blaine.

Blaine requires
more than one
eye.

He requires more
like nine.

Tanya goes outside
to smoke,

and I'm supposed to
make some dinner
for Blaine.

Blaine should eat
less meals from cans.
Less sugar.
Less red food coloring.

No soda!

This much I know.
But Tanya?

She just goes
outside to
smoke.

Recipe for Dinnertime at the McLeen Residence

Open one can of spaghetti.
Dump.
Microwave.
Wait.

Bowl for Blaine.
Bowl for me.
Two spoons.

One Sippy cup.
One bib.

(He doesn't really need
these, but I like
to try
to keep things
neat.)

Tell Blaine to stay at
the table.

Sit on sofa.
Turn on TV.

Eat.

Repeat.

AT LEAST ONE THING WANTS TO CLING TO TANYA

When Tanya comes in,
her clothes
(baggy, raggy sweats)
reek of smoke.

Cigarette odor—
L&M Menthol—
clings to her.

At least
one thing
wants to cling
to
Tanya.

THIS MESS

This is Dad's
second DUI,
and I don't know
why, but he
got assigned
to serve
forty-five
days
in county jail.

Last time,
there was just
a fine.
And probation.

(We even went
on that vacation!)

I picture him,
bummed, depressed.

But he got himself
into
this
mess.

Sometimes I Wonder

What would happen
to Blaine
if they both
died.

If Tanya and Dad
were killed, like in an
accident or something,
then who would
take care
of Blaine?

I'm thinking it would be
Me.

But what if
I had a husband or kids
or a career
or a trip to Spain …

Then

Who

Would

Take

Care

Of

Blaine?

I CAN'T WAIT FOR COLLEGE

I can't wait
to escape
this place.

I can't wait
for college.

Halls of knowledge!
Dorm room!
Freedom!

Nobody writing notes
of chores
with nothing
spelled
right!

But then
I remember
that Blaine
will be alone

with *them* ...

And what will
happen
to him then?

Doesn't he need me
to protect him
and inspect whether
he brushed his teeth?

Doesn't he need me
to sing to him
when their fights echo
too loud
at night?

Doesn't he need me
to make sure that he eats
a real breakfast?

It's not easy
being
the only one with
any brains ...

when it comes
to Blaine.

FREE MUSIC

Ms. Rose
tells me
there's a free
music program
for kids with incarcerated parents.

I could learn to play guitar.
Or drums.
Whatever.

Whatever I want!

I'd love to play drums,
but how am I going
to get there?

It's in the city,
Philly,
and there's no
way—with Blaine—

that Tanya
will be able

to take
me there.

She wouldn't want to
anyway.

The One from the Trailer

We live in a trailer
on Miami Road,
smack-dab in the middle of
Pennsylvania.
Tanya says we should call it
a mobile home.

It's a double-wide.
Whoop-de-do.
Big Friggin' Deal.

Who knew?

Well, one day
the bus driver, Gus,

said when I came
up the bus steps,

"Remind me who you are again.
Oh, that's right.

Never mind.
You're the one
from
the trailer."

Thanks, Gus.

The whole bus

got kind of

(awkward)
silent.

GONE

Music In My Room Is The Only Way I Can Escape.
Headset,

iPod,

and I'm gone.

Music In My Room Is The Only Way I Can Escape.

Green Day,

today,

and I'm gone.   i   am

                                    Gone.

Bada bing bada boom.

Music in my room.

THE DEAD BABY BEDROOM

I traded
rooms
with
Blaine,

The Day The Baby Died.

Blaine doesn't know
any better.
He doesn't
remember

his little sister … died

in there.

We burned
the crib and
turned
his room
into mine.

He has no idea
that he shares
his bedroom

with a dead
Baby
who never became
a real Girl.

FAMILY PUNCTUATION

I am a parenthesis
in this
family.*

                                        *(I'm a sidenote.)

Tanya is a comma,
and
Dad. Is. The. Period.

Carissa was—is?—a
question mark.

And Blaine … Well, Blaine …

He's
an
ellipsis
that

Goes

On …

And

On …

And

On …

…

…

…

…

…

…

LIFE EATS ME ALIVE

So we have family
punctuation,

and just once,
when Dad wasn't drunk,
(when he was on probation)

we actually took that family
vacation.
It was Baltimore:
the aquarium.

Sharks were the best part.

**Their razory teeth
reminded me
of the sharp**

shards eating up my heart.

**I WISH I COULD BE A killer SHARK
AND EAT OTHER PEOPLE'S HEARTS.**

**I got a shark tooth
necklace from the gift shop,**

**to remind me
that teeth—**

**and people and home and school and love and hate
and**

LIFE—

**Can eat me ...
alive.**

ONE SMALL WINDOW

In my teeny little bedroom,
and it looks out
at trees.

Trees,
gnarled, rough-trunked,
wave in the breeze.
Leaves change,
turn orange, amber,
golden, red.

I see
these trees from
my bed.

They seem
like friends.

I like
to open my
window

this time
of the year.

It smells
like a painting
by Norman Rockwell.

Leaves rustle,
dance almost,
in friendly little shimmies
of autumn whimsy.

I love these trees.
I love these leaves.

Except when they start to

    F

       a

          l

            l.

A MINIATURE FOREVER

Each and every day
is its own
Miniature Forever.

It can go
so long.
It can go
so wrong.

So much can happen.

Your life
can change
in just one second
of just one minute
of just one hour
of just one
single
day.

And that's what
happens
the day that

Blaine
just makes
up his mind
and decides
to
run
away.

OPTION NUMBER ONE

Blaine wakes,
pillow-crumple faced
from his nap,
and he stuffs his WWF backpack
with Fred the One-Eyed Teddy
Bear and a bunch
of other crap,
mostly toys.

He makes
a lot of noise,
and I ask him
what the heck
he thinks he's
doing.

"I go find Dad," he
announces, loud.
(Blaine has no
Inside Voice.)

His nose is dripping
snot as usual,
and half-moons of dirt

make each of Blaine's
fingernails
its own little
arc of finger garden.
(Sometimes I tease him
that he could grow tomatoes
or potatoes
in those
nails.)

We have three choices
for the question of Dad
when it comes to Blaine,
according to Tanya:

> 1. Dad is at work.
> 2. Dad is on an airplane in the sky.
> 3. Dad is visiting somebody we don't know.

So I go
with option number one.
"Dad is at work."

"You jerk," says Blaine.

Dad has been gone for eight days.

BOY GOES MISSING ON MIAMI ROAD

Says Channel 8
later that day.

"Autistic kids
often
run away,"
says Miss Bess.

"You were supposed
to be watching
your brother,"
says Tanya.

She is actually
the Mother.
(Just in case she forgets.)

"Don't panic.
We haven't lost one yet,"
says the cop.

"We'll help look.
We'll pray,"
say the neighbors.

WHAT THE NEWSPAPER SAYS

"Autistic Boy Missing,"
says
the headline
the next day.

I pick up the newspaper
from the table
and rip it into
tiny little shreds

of bad
news

I don't want
to
know.

THE FACEBOOK PAGE

Help Find Blaine McLeen
1,475 likes.   86 talking about this.

Community.

About:
Blaine is eight.
He went missing
in Chester County,
Pennsylvania,
on September 28th.

Blaine is learning-disabled,
and
he takes medication.

He was last seen
wearing a green T-shirt
with a turtle,
jeans,
and purple sneakers.

If you see
Blaine McLeen,
please
call
Pennsylvania State
Police
immediately.

1,475
Friends
Like
Help Find Blaine McLeen.

It's So Freaky

The way
that human bodies
just keep on
keeping on
when something tragic
happens.

We breathe.
We eat.
We pee.
We sleep.

Our brains know.
Our hearts know.

But somehow
our flesh and
blood and bones
and nose
don't know

anything
is
different.

WHAT IF

We don't find him
by Halloween?

What if
he's never seen
again?

What if …
he's …

Dead?

Yes, he's a pain.
Yes, he's insane.
Yes, he's Blaine.

But I just can't
wrap my head
around the idea

that I might never
see my brother

Again.

THE SEARCH

Everybody's helping
with the search.
They met at
the church.

Steeple
rising in between
all these
people.

The neighbors.
The cops.
The volunteer firemen.

Chloe King is here.
My guidance counselor,
Ms. Rose, is here too.

So is Morgan Reed, the pot queen,
and her big brother, Seth.

So is End of the World Girl
and her entire survivalist
family.
I wonder if they
could teach me how
to survive

If Blaine
has actually
died?

The Entire World Is Shouting His Name

We crunch through leaves,
below trees,
beside the creek,
flashlight beams
cutting deep.

"Blaine!" people shout
out.
BLAINE.

BLAINE.

It's as if the entire world
is yelling his name.

BLAINE.

SETH REED

Morgan Reed's big brother, Seth,
is walking by my side
holding the light,
and he's really nice.

I'm surprised that this guy
is the big bad pothead
I've heard about all over
school.

He seems really cool.

We're both wearing coats
because the night
has grown cold.

Seth holds
a low tree branch
so it won't
hit me.

He rips a root
from the ground
so I don't
trip.

He's *really* nice.
Big surprise.

But it's not right
that I'm even
thinking about how nice
this guy is …

When my little brother
is missing.

But still …

Seth Reed
Is Really
Sweet.

FOUND

"Found him! Got him!
We got him!"

The shouts echo
around
in my head, but
I can't tell from the sound
whether he's alive
or dead.

What if Blaine drowned
in the creek?

It's been a little bit over
one whole day
and one entire night.
What if he's dehydrated and
starving? Tired, he'd be
so tired.

Scared.

What if an animal of some kind
ate him alive?

I can't move.
I can't speak.
I can hardly breathe.

Seth puts his arm around me,
and we make our way …

TOWARD THE SOUND OF THE SHOUTS

A dozen flashlights,
maybe more,
pour yellow light
toward
the huge trunk
of a gnarly tree
beside the creek.

I cannot speak,
not one word.
I cannot even
breathe.

Blaine, asleep, his head
resting
on Fred
the One-Eyed
Teddy Bear.

His hair is a mess.

Is he asleep,
or could he be …

Blaine opens his eyes.
He looks surprised.

"Hi," he says.

Just
Hi.

WHEN DAD CALLS

There's a recorded voice
telling us that this call
might be recorded.

There's a pause.
Beeps.
Pause again.
Beeps again.

And then
Dad's voice,
so low. He doesn't know,
not yet.

He says, "Yo, what's up?"
Then
Tanya takes the phone

because she's decided

it's time
to tell him
about Blaine.

TANYA'S END OF THE CONVERSATION

"So, um, I didn't tell you when it
was happening, because, like,
it would be really crappy to
hear when you are in there.

It would have scared the crap out of you.

I'm not telling no joke.
Let me get a smoke."

(Tanya goes outside.
I stand at the kitchen window
to listen.)

"Well, the other day, Blaine,
he tried to run away."

...

"Yeah. We actually had
to call the police and all,
and it turned into this big search
that actually made the papers.

And the news on TV.
Almost caused me
to have a heart attack."

...

"Yeah. He's fine. They checked
him out at the hospital,
and he was just a little bit

dehydrated. Lucky he had two
bottles of Turkey Hill iced tea
in his backpack
and some peanut butter cheese crackers."

...

"Yeah. In the woods."

...

"Yeah. Good."

...

"Yeah. I would.

Well, Lexi was supposed to be
keeping an eye—"

...

"Fine."

...

"Yeah.
No."

...

"I know."

I SUCK

Not watching my brother.

I suck.
Not calling my mother.

I suck.
I wish I were another

person

who does not suck

so much.

NAGGING BLAINE

Ragging on him
again and again.

Never Ever Ever

Ever

Do That

Again.

DO.
    NOT.
        RUN.
            AWAY.

Ever.

Again.

The

End.

TANYA IS GIVING OFF A VIBE

Of blame,
accusation,

as if I cheated on
a game

I never intended
to play.

Now I Can Relate

To stories in the newspaper,
like the one that begins,
"Missing Woman Found After
10 Days."

I can relate
to stories on the TV,
like the one that ends,
"Little Girl Found Dead."

I can relate
to stories on the web,
like the one that says,
"Missing Man's Family Is
Frantic."

I can relate
in so many ways

to so many sad stories

now.

The Entire School Knows

About Blaine.
They know about Dad.

All the hidden
Secrets of Me

and my whacked-out
family

are now
in the
Public Domain.

Every day
feels like
rain.

SHE IS DRIVING ME CRAZY

I've been sixteen
for more than
three weeks,

and still Tanya has
not gotten
the hint
that I need

my driver's
permit.

I mention
Driver's Ed
and the nice discount
that we get
on car insurance.

I mention
my semi-friend Zelda

and how she just
got a used Toyota.

Duh.

Tanya still
doesn't get it.
Whatever.

She is driving
Me
Crazy.

BAD SEED

So I'm trying to carve
a pumpkin for Halloween,
at the same time
I'm trying to keep

Blaine from killing me
with the knife.

I tell him to chill out.
I tell him to sit down.
I tell him to back up.
I tell him to shut up.

I have to stop cutting
the face
because Blaine
wants to reach inside
to pull out
some pumpkin seeds.

"Bad seeds,"
Blaine says.

I'm a bad seed.

I wish that someone
could just reach
inside of me
and pull out those seeds

and carve a happy face
into me.

DAD IS HOME

Finally free,
but it still feels the same
to me.

Blaine is still
a pain.

Tanya is still
insane.

I am still
to blame

for everything.

TANYA HAS TO

Drive him to work.
She has to pick him up again.
I have to stay

with Blaine.

Every day,
we do it

Again.

IT'S BLAINE'S BIRTHDAY

Blaine's birthday
is more like a friggin'
circus than a birthday.

Tanya rented a dunk tank.
(It's like 63 degrees!)
She rented a snow cone machine.

Plus she had some Amish
guy driving a tractor
and pulling a wagon
full of hay and bratty little kids.

It's pathetic the way that Tanya
makes a big friggin' deal out of
Blaine's birthday …

But never,
ever,
ever
mine.

I NEVER DID GET THOSE
FREE MUSIC LESSONS

Because I guess
Tanya forgot.

There's a lot
that Tanya forgets
(like, for example,
my dentist appointment
when my tooth hurt
for more
than a month).

But she never lets
me forget
what happened

the day
that Blaine
ran away.

Most People Are Thankful at Thanksgiving

I wish I could be
thankful.

Yeah, Dad's home,
sitting in the same old
broken recliner,
watching the same old
reality shows on TV.

This is reality
for me.

MEAT FREAKS ME OUT

Turkey grease
drips and sizzles
from the poor doomed
bird
in the oven.

Cooking meat
freaks
me out.

I think I'm becoming
a vegetarian
like Miss Fipps,
the librarian
at school.
She's so cool.
Maybe if I don't
eat meat, I can be
cool too.

Miss Fipps has at least
eight tattoos, all of them
from famous children's books.

On her arm:
Where the Wild Things Are.

On the other arm:
Harold and the Purple Crayon.

I wonder what Miss Fipps
is doing
for Thanksgiving,
and if her family is
dysfunctional.

Like mine.

TANYA'S HEATING UP

Frozen mashed potatoes
and canned yams.
The trailer
would smell kind of good,

if you could
just ignore the wet smell
of Blaine's disposable
diaper.

That boy
is way too
hyper.

GRAY DAYS

I hate
the way
gray days
at the end
of November
shade more gray
into December.

Expectations are way
too high in December.

It's like
everybody expects to have
a happy
family

and get everything
on their Christmas
list,

and that their wishes
will all come true.

That is *so* not true.

That is why I paint
holidays

Blue.

PART TWO:

THE WINTER

A BRAND-NEW YEAR

Thank God
the holidays
are done.

It's past
January 1.

A brand-new
year is
here.

Whoopee.
Great.

Confetti, glittery ball
falling, shimmery midnight
kisses on TV …
All over.

Do I dare to hope
that this year
will be a better one
than the one before,
or the ten before
that one?

ONCE UPON A TIME

There was me,
a teensy bit of
a princess, a diva,
a weensy Queen
of the World.

This was when I
was little,
when I lived with Mom
and her mom,
my grandmom.

Confident, outgoing,
outspoken,
I knew I was cool.

Tutus and tiaras,
pink froufrou,
a Band-Aid for every
booboo.

Girly-girl in training.
Brave enough
to wear stuff
that got me noticed.

Now, I just try to blend.
Not to stand out.

I used to be a magnolia—flashy-
open—like the ones that grow
at Mom's house.

Now, I'm more of a lotus, closed,
underwater in a scum-coated pond.
A locust,

too scared
to come out of my
shell.

THE ROPE

In a game of parental
tug-of-war,
I decided
when I was five
to stop trying
to survive.

I just let them
yank.

Back and forth,
forth and back.

There and here,
here and there.

Nowhere
really feels
like home,

And I don't know
where I
belong.

WHEN I WENT TO THE MEGA-CHURCH WITH GRANDMOM

Hope filled me up.
My cup was actually
almost
half full. No bull.

I had friends there,
at the mega-church,
which was more like
a rock concert
than a church service,
with its lasery lights
and quivering electric instruments.

School was cool.
I had friends there too.

But then I moved …

And I had to wrap
my head around
who I was.

I'M A GEEK

Sixteen
and never been kissed.
Never been missed.

Romance.
Lips touch lips.
Teeth click teeth.
Heartbeats meet.

(Among other things.)

And it all seems
way too awkward
to me.

But then again,
I am
a geek.

I wonder if
anybody will ever
want to kiss

Me?

IF ONLY I COULD DRIVE

I could get a job.

If only I could drive,
I could get *a w a y*.

If only I could drive,
I'd feel as if I could fly.

If only I could drive,
I'd leave them all behind.

I'd hit the   R
                            O
                            A
                            D

and just go
and go
and   G
                            O

Tanya Is a High School Dropout

No emphasis
for education,
that's Tanya.

She quit school
in the tenth grade
and never went
back
again.

She married Dad,
had Blaine,
and got me.

Can't they see
what a waste of brain space
it is
to be the way
they are?

They can't even afford
a second car.

Me? I will reach
for the stars.
I will achieve.
I will get a college degree,
even if it kills me.

Because there's no way
I want to end
up anything
like
them.

Toys Litter the Yard

Outside our trailer
it is a junkyard
of Big Wheels and
broken trucks
and other stuff,

as if an entire
plastic blizzard
of toy litter
piled high
one winter's day
and never melted away.

Why don't they
make Blaine
clean up after
he plays?

We do have
a garage
where that barrage
of junk
could go.

But no.

I think they
think if
people driving by
see piles of toys,
they will
think,

Oh, those people
who live in that trailer
must really love their
kid because just look
how much money
they spend on him!

Not.
I have news for them.

It makes our whole
family look like
Trash.

They Have No Passion

For anything
except stuff
they can buy.

Junk
they can
leave
all over
the yard

so that we all
look like a bunch
of morons.

Sometimes in the Morning

Before school
I pretend that
the narrow hallway
in our trailer
is Death Row,

and I am walking
the Green Mile
on this pukey-green
carpet,

destined for the electric chair.

Dead Girl Walking.

Lethal injection
by Section 77
of the tenth grade
at Lakeview High School.

I am
screwed.

Somebody Stacked My Locker

Blocks of wood
fall
on my head.

There's a note
on the door that says,
"Got You Again,
Trailer Trash
Redneck
Blockhead."

I slam the metal
door, kick the wooden
blocks across the floor,
rip the note to shreds.

TRAILER TRASH
REDNECK
BLOCKHEAD

to the rescue
of myself
once again.

ART CLASS IS USUALLY THE BEST

But
today we have a test.

I forget
where Rembrandt was
born and why Van Gogh
did no
famous paintings
of corn.

I get an F.

In art!

Mr. Hart
just shakes his head
as he makes the big red
slash of angry
F
on my paper.

I drop an
f-bomb
in my head.

I guess
I'm
a disappointment

to everybody.

In the Girls' Room

In between classes
I clean my glasses.
Take a swipe at my face
with a wet paper

towel.

Yowza.
I look like somebody
who just flunked
a test.

A mess.

Hair frizzed,
couple of zits,
three acne pits.

An unnecessary mess,

that's me.

But then again,
if I knew a
different way to be …

That wouldn't be

me.

When I Go to See Ms. Rose

Her door is closed.

An orange sign,
Magic Markered in black:

STUDENTS WHO USUALLY
SEE MS. ROSE
WILL NOW BE ASSIGNED
TO MR. GOLDSTEIN.

UNTIL FURTHER NOTICE
MS. ROSE IS ON EXTENDED LEAVE
OF ABSENCE.

My heart tumbles,
bounces down the hall.

Ms. Rose
is the only
one I am comfortable
enough to
confide in.

She knows most
of the Secrets of Me,
and they don't even
freak her
out.

What will I do now
without
Ms. Rose?

Health Is Next

And it includes
sex ed.

Kids whisper, giggle,
act as if
they are ten again
in sex ed.

"Did you hear?" says
Chloe King
as I sit down.

"Amanda Brown
is pregnant.
Knocked up
by that dude
who's locked up
for robbing
the WaWa store."

Chloe King says this as if
it is hot gossip,
as if it is cool news,
just like the time
she bragged she passed out
from too much booze.

Chloe King needs to
get a life.

And Amanda Brown
has no idea
about the kind of life

she is bound
to give that
kid.

School Is a Blur

The rest of the day.

It feels like I'm on a
fast circle of an
amusement park
ride and can't get off,
even if I call out
for the ride to
Stop.

I wonder what
would happen
if I just hopped

off?

BEEP. BEEP. BEEP.

I can't seem
to not oversleep.
The beep-beep-beep
of the alarm
on my clock
just goes
into my dreams,
and I keep sleeping.

I've missed the bus
a bunch of times,
and Tanya is ticked.

She says she's got enough
stuff, what with driving
Dad and taking care of
Blaine, and there's no
way she's going to take me
to school
and waste all that gas
when there's a bus,

and we pay enough taxes
for me to ride that bus
every day for the rest of
my life,
blah-blah-blahs.

I don't know what to do.

It's not like I'm trying
to miss the bus.

It's just
that I can't seem
to not
oversleep.

It's winter.
Snow and toys are deep.   Beep. Beep. Beep.

9/11 IS THE DISCUSSION SUBJECT

In history,
and it's a mystery
to me why we need
to keep dwelling upon
all that sadness
from the past.

Airplanes into buildings,
towers into flames.
People jumping as if
they had wings.

Everything burned to
ashes and dust.
Just dust
and ashes.

It reminds me of a Bible
verse from the mega-church.

I have a migraine
from thinking about 9/11
and why all those people
died and left for heaven.

I don't want to think so much
about the dustiness
of us.

YOU KNOW THAT KID PIG-PEN

From the old
Charlie Brown
and Snoopy cartoons?

The one who walks
around with a cloud
of dust
floating after him.

Well, I have news for
you. Pig-Pen is us,
all of us, every freaking
one of us!

Because we all shed
so many dead
skin cells into the air.

They are invisible, but
they are there,
floating around each
one of us
like a Pig-Pen-ish
cloud of dust.

Dust
Is
Us.

I PASS GAS IN SCIENCE CLASS

Silently,
but it is
Deadly.

DeeAnne Smedly,
(this cheerleader chick)
sniffs and says,
"What reeks?"

"Lexi McLeen,"
says Morgan Reed.

She waves her
hand before her face,
chasing away
the reek of me.

I used to wish
that farts would come
out as puffs of colored
clouds so that we could
know who passed gas.

But now, in science class,
I'm glad
there is no
colored gas cloud
around me,

because Lexi McLeen
is already
a Freak.

SO WE'RE ON THE SUBJECT OF EARTHQUAKES AND NATIONAL WEATHER TRAGEDIES

And End of the World Girl
says that she believes

everybody needs
to stock up on wheat,

just in case
an attack happens.

"I don't mind helping people,"
she says. "But I resent

having to help those
who could have prepared,

but just didn't

care."

That Night

I'm telling
Tanya and Dad
about how
End of the World Girl
says we need
to get some wheat
and be
prepared.

We need to care.

As usual, they just
laugh, making fun
of me. I am the joke
of this family.

"Seriously, we need
wheat," I say.

"Seriously, you need
some normal friends,"
says Dad.

No kidding.

THE NEXT DAY

In life skills class,
Mrs. Haas
is sitting on an
enormous box
from Fed-Ex.
I wonder if this is
going to be
about sex.

"Guess what
I have for each one
of you?" she says
with a wrinkly grin.

I have no clue.

"Ta-da!" Mrs. Haas
announces as she
flings open the
lid.

She pulls out a ... doll?

"The Almost-Real Baby!" she
says, acting as thrilled as
if she just gave birth.

MRS. HAAS BLAH-BLAH-BLAHS

All about how
the Almost-Real Baby
has electronic monitors,
and it will record everything we
do. (Or don't do, as the case may be.)

These things will cry and cry
if they don't get every single thing they need.
And apparently they need a lot.

The dolls need to be fed and changed
and burped and rocked. Kept the
exact right temperature. Not too cold,
not too hot.

It's like an electronic
Pain-in-the-Butt
Robot.

MRS. HAAS HANDS THE DOLLS OUT

At random.
And I get …
A girl.

Just what
I didn't want.

It has a face
like Carissa Grace.

It's wearing pink,
just like she did.

It has dimples
and a wisp of hair,
and it's soft and cuddly
in a bubblegum-colored sleeper.

It even smells
like a baby.

Like Carissa Grace.

I try to swallow
this emotion, but
a whole ocean of sadness
washes over me.

I now have
my very own

Teeny Little Grief Machine.

THE SEVEN SUCKY THINGS

So,
in one winter week,
these are the seven sucky
things that happened to
me:

1. My locker was stacked … again.
2. I overslept … again.

3. I failed an art test. An F!

4. My guidance counselor bailed.
5. I passed gas in science class.

6. I got an Almost-Real Baby that I really don't want.
7. End of the World Girl wouldn't stop talking about wheat.

Oh, and today I have a brand-new zit.

Sweet.

163

LEXI-RHYMES-WITH-SEXY
IS SHOWING HER LEGS

"Oh, look,"
says Chloe King.

"Lexi-Rhymes-with-Sexy
is showing her legs!"

Awesome.

I decide for once
in my life
to wear a skirt
to school,
and what do I
get?

"Lexi-Rhymes-with-Sexy
is showing her legs."

You can't even see
flesh.

I'm wearing white tights,
kind of like leggings,
almost.

Chloe King
is toast.

WHOA

I place my baby
in the locker
so I don't shake
her head around
while I'm
flipping out
on Chloe King.

"Why do you always
have to freaking pick
on me?" I scream.

"Whoa," says Chloe King.
She backs away, puts her
hands up, as if I have a gun
or something.

"Chill out," she says.
"It was just a joke."

Kids are staring.
Half the hallway has slowed.

"Whoa, Lexi. Can't you take
a joke?"

I take a deep breath.
Pick up the creepy Almost-Real Baby again.

I wish I had something
to smoke.

I wish I had somebody
to choke.

No joke.

I Wonder If Anybody Ever Runs Away from a Fake Baby

The fake baby
is crying in my arms
when I get back
to my locker.

I suck at being a
mom.

This thing is
beyond annoying.

I smack—I mean
pat—its back.

The diaper is wet …
Again.

It's whining because
it's hungry …

Again.

This being-a-mother
thing is *so* not
fun.

I wonder if anybody
ever runs away
from a fake
baby?

WHEN I PASS AMANDA BROWN

In the hallway,
I hold up my
fake baby
and I say,

"I hope you're
ready for this."

She holds up
her fake baby:
a boy.

"I have one too,
don't forget," she says.

"Yeah, but you also
have one inside of you.
A real one.

And you totally have no
clue what you
being a teenage
mom is going to do

to that baby's entire
rest of its life.

Just look at me
if you need an
example."

Amanda Brown
just tucks her
fake baby away,
and her face
is kind of gray.

Sucks to be
her too.

DIG THE DRESS

I pass Amanda Brown
later, and she acts
as if we didn't already
connect. Pretending is
what some people do
best.

She calls out,
"Hey, Lexi-Rhymes-with-Sexy,
I dig the dress."

"Thanks," I mutter.
It's a skirt.
Duh.

Maybe being with child
makes some girls
dumb.

I hope that Amanda Brown
somehow becomes a whole lot
smarter
before she brings that baby
into the world.

I hope she and that dude
aren't rude to one another,
and that they don't yank
back and forth
when it comes to their kid.

Fake babies
aren't the only ones
to complain.
Little kids feel pain too,
you know.

I want to go
home and change
my clothes.

In Life Skills Class

Mrs. Haas asks
how everybody is
doing with their babies.

Nobody answers.
We're all too busy jiggling
our kids so they don't throw
a conniption fit.

"A lot of work, isn't it?" Mrs. Haas says.
"Having a baby is twenty-four/seven."

"Mine is so annoying," says Morgan Reed.

Yeah, right.
It bites
not being able to smoke weed
around your electronic baby,
who'd register the smoke.

Morgan Reed would be so busted
if she smoked weed.

Listen to me. I'm acting like I'm the Queen
of Goody-Goodyness.

What a joke.
I'm wishing I could smoke
too.

I'm going to paint this baby
a really ugly
shade of blue,

even though it's supposed
to be a girl.

Pink stinks.
It makes me think too much.

After School

I go in my room.
I get out my
best oil pastels,
and I choose
a shade of blue
somewhere in
between Summertime
Sky
and Dead-Person
Skin.

I take off the fake
baby's pink hat
and its pink sleeper,

and I paint that baby
over most of its
body
in that strange shade
of blue.

BLUE BOY POOP

You know
that Off Broadway show
"Blue Man Group"?

That's my fake baby
now.

It is no longer a girl.

It is a boy …
Blue.

The diaper is full.

This is my new

project:

Blue
Boy
Poop.

THE NEXT DAY

In life skills class,
Mrs. Haas asks,

"Lexi, what on earth
did you do to your
baby girl?"

"I painted it so that
it is now a
boy," I reply.

Everybody stares,
and there's a tight
quiet in the room,
like the inside
of a womb.

Swoosh. Swoosh.
I can hear my own
heart pumping blood.

Next Thing You Know

I'm in the guidance counselor's
office, but it's not my guidance
counselor. It's Mr. Goldstein.

Fine.

I cross my arms.
I close my eyes.

Fine.

I just won't talk.
I'll walk.

Can somebody please
take this stupid crying
baby?

Its name is
Blue Boy Poop,

just so you have
the scoop.

I Throw the Fake Baby

On the floor.

I walk out the door.

I walk really fast,
but I can still hear

the baby.

It is crying.

Fine.

I go back inside.

I pick it up.
I shut it up.

I don't want to
flunk

life skills.

So Mr. Goldstein Calls My House

But nobody answers.
Tanya's probably too
busy with Miss Bess
and my holy mess of
a real little brother.

He leaves a message.

But what Mr. Goldstein
doesn't know is this:

They
Never
Call
Anybody
Back.

I DECIDE THAT NIGHT

To live up
to my nickname.

Lexi-Rhymes-with-Sexy
will show some leg.

She will show
them.

And maybe
I will even sleep

with Seth Reed.

Sweet.

THE NEXT MORNING

Dead Girl Walking
is showing some serious
skin.

Yeah, it's winter.
I'm already freezing
from the inside out,
so what does it matter?

Seriously high skirt.
Seriously low shirt.
Fishnets.

Flesh
is the new

black.

WHEN I GET ON THE BUS

Gus says,

"If you were my daughter,
I'd send you home
to change your clothes."

End of the World Girl says,

"You have some eyeliner
on your nose."

Some kid I don't know says,

"That baby looks stupid painted
blue."

I ignore Gus.
I ignore the kid I don't know.

I ignore End of the World Girl.

Ignoring
Boring
People
Is My
New
Modus
Operandi.

BUT I CAN'T IGNORE MR. GOLDSTEIN

Because he says
that if my parents
don't answer the phone,
he will have to call
in some
mental health
professionals.

"Could you try to call home
from your cell phone?"
he asks.

My lips are frozen
together. I can't open
my mouth.

So I just write it
down,
and I write it
LOUD:

I DON'T HAVE MY OWN PHONE.

NEXT THING YOU KNOW

I'm being evaluated.
De-valuated.

Re-evaluated.

"Do you ever have thoughts of harming yourself?"
"Is anyone hurting you?"
"Is anything bothering you?"
"Have you ever attempted to hurt yourself?"

I tell them,

"Yes. I am depressed, I guess.
I took Tylenol that time.

I cut myself but not with a knife.

Welcome to my life."

They Need to Keep Me

For a couple of days.
That's okay.

The fake baby is gone
anyway.

I have nothing to do
but sleep

and pray.

Everything will be okay.

They need to keep
me

for a couple of days.

WHEN I FINALLY OPEN UP

Stuff pours out of
me like water.

I'm a broken
dam, flooding words.

It's like my bloody
clogged-up, bogged-down
heart has been opened,
and I'm pumping stuff
into the air.

Emotional surgery.

I talk about my
so-called
family,
and about how
I am just a sidenote,
a parenthesis.

I talk about
Blaine, and the way
he makes me crazy.

I talk about Tanya,
and how much I hate
her, and she hates me
in this so-called family.

I talk about how Dad
went to jail, and about how
he drinks too much, and about
how I just wish he would hug—
maybe even tell me he loves me—
once in a while.

I talk about the piles of toys,
the trailer, and
the way the kids at school
tease me.

How Blaine went missing,
and it was all because of me.

How my baby sister died
in her sleep in her crib
in my room over a year ago,
in autumn.

And maybe that was
because of me too.

How I painted that fake baby
blue.

How Dad told me Mom
was a stripper, and how
they always talk bad about
one another, and how I try
to just forget about whoever it is
I'm not living with

because it just hurts too much
to remember.

How I wish that the teenage pregnancy
that turned out to be me
had just ended with another option.

How once upon a time
there was me,
and I had a different way
to be in this
world.

Why Mom lives in Alabama
with her brand-new family,
and how it's so far away
from me.

All the stuff that happened
to me in just one
year … just one week …
just one freaking day!

How I've been tick-tocking
away
like a clock
or a bomb,
just waiting
to explode.

196

And now that I've

exploded,

when can I
ever
go home?

It's Snowing

Outside.

Through the
hospital window,

I try to watch
the white flakes
drifting, sifting

slow,

but I can't watch
for long.

I keep falling

asleep.

WHEN I FINALLY OPEN MY EYES

I feel a little bit
like Dorothy in
The Wizard of Oz.
The tornado has stopped.
My house has plopped
down.

I am surrounded by
a half circle of
people, apparently
watching me sleep.

There's Tanya …
and Mom?!
Dad. Grandma!

Even Blaine, and he's

silent and still
for once in his life,
sucking his thumb,
staring.

"Hi," I say.

Just
Hi.

PART THREE:

THE SPRING

THIS IS HOW I FEEL TODAY

Did you ever notice
how completely
brand new you
feel on the first warm
day after a long, cold
winter?

The kind of blue-sky,
bird-chirpy,
flower-bud-
after-a-rain
day when you notice
the smell of spring
in your nose

and the tickle of new grass
between your toes.

You know that feeling of
surprise sunshine on your face
on that first warm day,

and how you breathe deep
because every freaking thing
smells so fresh, like starting over?

Well, this is how I feel today,
now that I am finally, finally
okay.

Yay.

EVERYBODY IN SCHOOL KNOWS

My entire story,
including the hospital stay,

but they also know
that now I'm okay.

It's all right.
Life doesn't bite
all the time
anymore.

I feel as if I've
been off to fight,
serving in a personal
inside-of-me
war.

It tore me
up from the inside out,
but now I'm all about

Being Okay.

WELCOME BACK, LEXI MCLEEN

Says Seth Reed.
He gives me
a big friggin'
movie-theater pack
of peanut M&M'S.

"How did you know that
I love these?" I ask Seth Reed,
ripping open the box.
"You rock!"

"I like to read
your Facebook posts," says Seth.
"And that's how I know
most things about you."

I tell him it's true,
I do love peanut M&M'S,
especially
the blue.

I might be falling
in love
with Seth Reed
too.

SETH REED IS CLEAN

He quit smoking weed.
He stopped selling pot.

Seth Reed is clean,
and—wow—is he ever sweet.

I think I might be
falling head over feet
for Seth Reed.

His eyes are green.
His hair black and shaggy.

He's like crack,
and I can't stop thinking
about Seth Reed.

The Librarian, Miss Fipps

Flips out when she sees me.
"Lexi!" she screams.
She hustles over and wraps
me in a big hug
with those *Wild Things-*
Purple Crayon book arms.

Miss Fipps tells me that she
has been thinking of me, and
how she read some of my poetry,
and how I'm so talented, really,
and that I should think about
being a writer or an artist,
because I'm so naturally
creative.

She points behind my head,
up high, and there hangs
one of my paintings that I
did in art class one day:
the face of Carissa Grace,
blurry and soft blue and so full
of memories and love.

"Awww," I say. "That was my
baby sister I painted that day."

"Beautiful," announces Miss Fipps.
"And so are you, Lexi.
I am happy to have you
back in school."

Me too.

MISS FIPPS TELLS ME

About a brand-new
after-school book club
that she is just starting.

"We'll all read the same book
and then we'll discuss it,"
she says. "We also plan to
write poetry and paint
in relation to the stories
we read."

Sweet.

Count me in.

It is time to begin

a brand-new

way to be

in this

school.

It's the First Meeting

Of the book club,
which includes kids
from Lakeview High
but also other kids from
other places. Whoever
wants to come. Whoever
just loves reading and poetry
and art.

I am part of this
Cool Group.

There's one dude
who is new. Somebody
I never saw before. And
something about the guy
makes it hard for my eyes
to look away from his face.
Blue eyes, curly long hair,
Led Zeppelin T-shirt. Ripped jeans.
Red Converse sneakers.

We go around the room
and say our names and a little
bit about ourselves.
"Lexi McLeen, sixteen," I say.
"I love to read. I love music.
I love poetry and painting.
And I'm a vegetarian."

When it comes to the new dude,
he says, "Max Batter. Seventeen. Homeschooled.
I love music too. I play bass in a band.
And, um, I like a lot of stuff. Especially
good books and nice people who don't suck."

Everybody laughs, and I think,
Hello, Max Batter!

And somehow, my obsession with Seth Reed
doesn't matter.

Seth Who?

Funny how crushes
can change so much
from one
day to the next. One
minute to the next!
Somebody new walks
into a room and *BOOM*!
Crush busted
out all over.

With somebody you never even knew
existed.

This guy
is so freaking cool.
He's so hot.
He is *so* not
a dork.
He is definitely the best
boy in the entire library,
maybe even in the entire
world.

I dig his face.
I like his voice.
I like his smile.
I love his eyes.

I am literally high …

on the intoxicating
fumes from
across the room

… of Max Batter.

AFTER THE BOOK CLUB MEETING

Max Batter comes up to me!
"Hey," he says.
"Hey," I say.

OMG, he's even better up close.
I love his nose.
And his teeth.

Good grief! What is happening to me?!

Now I know what it means
to be weak in the knees.

To be butterfly fluttery in the gut.

"Miss Fipps told me
that you play the drums,"
he says.

"Um, well, not exactly. I mean,
I used to play the
snare back in eighth grade
in the marching band, but
then I quit. I really want to play a drum kit,
though."

"If you can play the snare,
you can learn, easy," he says.
"Just add bass drum on the right foot,
high-hat pedal on the left,
a few cymbals, tom-toms, and ta-da.
Drumming!"

"Oh-kay," I say.

"Our band is new," says Max Batter.
"And we really need a
drummer. A girl drummer would be cool.
I could teach you
most days after school."

"Cool," I say. "Okay," I say.
"That would be awesome," I say.
"Amazing," I say.

Somehow, my mouth pronounces words,
while my heart
chirps like a zillion hyper birds.
A bazillion birds with ADHD.

It doesn't suck
to be
Me.

MAX BATTER HANDS ME HIS CELL PHONE

He says,
"Here. Text your
'rents. Tell them
you'll be playing
drums at my house.
Tell them it's okay.
I'm safe. Not a serial
killer."

"Wow," I say.
"I feel so much better now."

I smile,
take Max Batter's phone,
and text home:

I'M OK.
No worries.
Going to new
friend's house.

I grin,
feeling sneaky
as a mouse.

MAX BATTER'S CAMARO

Is vintage:
gleamy black
with hot orange
flicker flames.

"Sweet ride!"
I smile.

"Thanks," says
Max. "I painted it
myself plus restored
parts that needed it."

Max opens the door
for me, and my
heart flings open
too.

This is like a
dream come true.

I climb inside,
where it smells
like pine tree
air freshener
and french fries
and some kind of guy
cologne.

Breathing deep,
I say again,
"Sweet."

And then I just
sink into the seat.

MAX IS A FINE DRIVER

We glide,
or so it seems
to me.

Smooth, practically
floating on road
that feels more
like sky.

I am high
on Max Batter.
He is one cool
dude.

I sneak glances
at his profile,
which only makes
me smile
even more.

I think my cheeks
might crack
with happiness.

BADA BING BADA BOOM

There's happiness in the room.
I'm drumming,
and my entire being
is humming
with something
like love.

My heart
thumps along
with the drums.

My smiles—laughs!—
are cymbal crashes.

Max Batter is grinning,
and my world is spinning
in a whole new
direction.

I sit upon the drum throne,
and I forget all about home,
and I am the queen.

And there are no more teeny little
grief machines
inside of me.

I am fine.

My life
is
mine!

Bada bing bada boom.
There's happiness
in this room.

I look through
the window,
and it's out there

too.

Max Is Driving Me Home

I think about telling him
some address other than
Miami Road.

But no.
He needs to know
the whole truth:
the
Story of Me.

How I don't live
in a perfect home
with a perfect family.

How I sometimes feel
like a failure
inside of that trailer …
and on the
outside too.

How I am just a girl
who hurts.

I blurt
out to Max
all of the facts
of
my entire
freaky life,

from Mom to Dad
and everything
in between
for Lexi McLeen.

I tell Max
about the time
I carved
H-A-T-E
on my arm,
and how I had
to go
to the Funny Farm.

I tell him about

Carissa Grace,
and how
I can still see her face,
and that's
why
I have to
paint.

I tell him about
the fake baby,
and how maybe
I was crazy
because I painted it blue.

I also tell him
about
Dad going to jail,
and how
I sometimes wish
I could just bail
on this whacked-
out family
of mine.

I tell Max Batter
about Blaine—

how he drives
me insane
and is such
a total pain,
but how much
I love him
anyway.

I tell him about
the day
that Blaine
ran away,
and how
I thought I'd pay
for the rest
of my existence.

I tell him about
smoking weed,
and about how
I actually liked
Seth Reed,
and about
End of the World
Girl
and the
counselor, Ms. Rose,

who saved
my life.

I even tell Max
about how
I might like
to be some
nice guy's wife
one day—maybe—
far, far away.

Maybe after
I go to Spain.
And learn
how to deal
with rain.
And figure out
how not
to be a
major pain.

"When I grow
up, though,
I know
I'll make my own
life

way different
from how
they
made theirs."

Max just listens.
His blue eyes
glisten.

I so wish
I could kiss him.

DID YOU EVER NOTICE

How the inside
of a car
can feel like
an entire galaxy
that consists
of only you
and him.

The inside of a car
can feel like
a star so far,
far away
from everything
below.

Now I know
how it feels
to live inside
a snow dome:
just you and him
and nothing else
anywhere …
but inside a car.

Max Reaches Over

And takes my hand.
Our thumbs dance.

This must be
romance.

MAX PULLS INTO OUR DRIVEWAY

Tanya is on the porch,
smoking, of course.

Dad is mowing the lawn,
holding a beer,
steering
in between
Big Wheels and
other crap.

Blaine is acting
crazy,
as usual, running
and jumping,
dumping buckets
of water
all around
the clutter
of toys.

So much
noise.

Dad tips the
beer can.
Tanya blows
a cloud
of smoke.

"Are you sure
you really want
to meet them?"
I ask Max,
only half-joking.

Tanya just keeps on
smoking.

Dad just keeps on
mowing.

Blaine just keeps on
being Blaine.

The air smells
like gasoline.

Max looks at me.
He's so sweet.
I could sink deep
into those eyes.

"Why wouldn't I?" he
replies.
"Let's do this."

He lifts
my hand
to
his lips
for a quick
little kiss.

"I hope
you're up
for this,"
I whisper.

My heart
is ticking, tocking,
beating, leaping,

keeping the time
of me
and my life.

Max nods.
"I'm ready,"
he says.

"Let's go," I say.
"Hey," I say to Blaine.

There is nothing to explain.
No apologies to be made.

The sun is beginning to fade.
There's a sliver of springtime moon,
a slight sparkling
of stars.

"Hi, Blaine," Max says.
He gives my brother
a fist bump.

Dad turns off the mower.
Tanya walks over.
She blows smoke
and I almost choke,
but then there's
also the nice smell
of fresh-cut grass.

"Tanya, Dad, this is Max."

"Nice to meet you," says Max.

Max reaches out his hand.
Dad does too.

I won't paint
this scene
blue.

The true shades
of this magical
day
are kind of like a
beautiful fire,
or like a setting sun:
pink, violet,
sinking below
the horizon
that is always
in my sight.

Tonight
it will grow
dark,
but there are
always
the stars,
and the moon
can shine
too.

Tomorrow
will always
come,
and I can always
rely on
the sun.

Every tomorrow
brings
another chance
for us all
to win.

The world
continues
to spin.

LINDA OATMAN HIGH

Linda Oatman High is an author, a playwright, and a journalist who lives in Lancaster County, Pennsylvania. She holds an MFA in writing from Vermont College and presents writing workshops and assemblies for all ages. In England in 2012, Linda was honored with the *Sunday Times* EFG Short Story Award shortlist. Her books have won many awards and honors. Information on her work may be found online at www.lindaoatmanhigh.com.